THE

DRAGON
HUNTER'S

HANDBOOK

by Lori Summers

PSSI
PRICE STERN SLOAN

www.quirkproductions.com

Designed by Paul Kepple and Timothy Crawford @ Headcase Design

Published by Price Stern Sloan, a division of Penguin Putnam Books for Young
Readers, New York.

PSS! is a registered trademark of Penguin Putnam Inc.

Printed in Singapore.

Library of Congress Catalog Card Number: 2001089181

ISBN: 0-8431-7704-7

A B C D E F G H I J

PHOTOGRAPHY CREDITS

Pg. ii: Everett Collection

Pg. x: Everett Collection

Pgs. 12–13: Everett Collection

Pg. 22: Everett Collection

Pg. 24: Kobal Collection

Pg. 27: Jim Zuckerman/Corbis

Pg. 29: Art Resource, NY

Pg. 31: Historical Picture
Archives/Corbis

Pg. 32: Bettmann/Corbis

Pg. 33: Courtesy of The Greater
Alton/Twin Rivers Convention and
Visitors Bureau

Pg. 35: (top three) SuperStock;
(bottom three) Kennan Ward/Corbis,
Jonathan Blair/Corbis, Photofest

Pg. 36: Photofest

Pg. 44: Everett Collection

Pgs. 52–53: Photofest

Pg. 56: Photofest

Pgs. 62–63 (dragons) Photofest;
(trees) SuperStock

Pg. 65: Kobal Collection

THE

DRAGON
HUNTER'S

HANDBOOK

CONTENTS

INTRODUCTION

Have you ever walked past an abandoned house and wondered where all the people went? Have you ever visited a forest and seen several trees in a row that looked like they'd been toppled over by some massive force? Have you ever wondered why some buildings have scorch marks that reach up as high as the twentieth floor?

Many people find ordinary, everyday explanations for this sort of physical evidence: People sometimes just move away, strong winds can overturn trees, and fires can happen any time, especially in large cities.

A select few, however, will look more closely at the clues and wonder if there's more to it all than meets the eye. This special group is trained to put the facts together, plot out a pattern, and come up with an answer to an often overlooked question: Could a *dragon* be behind all of this?

These specially trained experts are known as Dragon Hunters, and they have been hard at work protecting the world for centuries.

Most Dragon Hunters learned their trade from the generations of hunters that came before them. But now, *The Dragon Hunter's Handbook* can teach you everything you need to know so that you, too, can become a successful

Dragon Hunter. You'll learn all about the places where dragons like to live, the foods they like to eat, and the objects they like to collect. You'll learn that not all dragons are mean, nasty creatures, and that you can even become friends with one!

The dragon's fascinating history is mixed with the stuff of myths and legends, but many of these legends have a basis in fact. This book will teach you the information you can count on: how to recognize a dragon when you see one and what to do if the dragon is not inclined to be friendly.

When a town is at a dragon's mercy, you'll be the one to get the call. From damsels in distress to frightened townspeople, everyone will be glad you've taken the time to learn to be a Dragon Hunter. Keep a fire extinguisher handy, and good luck!

BECAUSE A DRAGON IS A CURIOUS CREATURE, IT MAY WANT TO EXAMINE *YOU* JUST AS MUCH AS YOU WANT TO EXAMINE *IT*

CHAPTER ONE

EXAMINING THE DRAGON

The traditional dragon is a familiar image: a large, scaly, fire-breathing monster. But although many dragons do fit this description, the image isn't entirely accurate.

All dragons have wings, fangs, and claws—just as people have arms, teeth, and nails. But people have different hair and eye colors, which make them unique. Dragons also have characteristics that can make them look different from other dragons in their families, like their brothers or sisters.

They may have scales, fur, or rough skin like a shark. They may be large or small. Not all dragons breathe fire, and not all of them can fly.

There are some traits that all dragons do have, however. A dragon's primary characteristics include the following: wings, large-fanged teeth, a long tail, eyes that face forward, a spiny backbone, short arms, and clawed fingers.

If the animal in question has the traits mentioned above, it's probably a dragon, which is a species unlike any other. It *can* be confusing, however: Two dragons may look different and yet both be dragons. But think of it this way: A Chihuahua and a Great Dane don't look alike at all, yet they're both dogs. (Of course, a dragon the size of a Chihuahua or a Great Dane wouldn't be much of a challenge for a fully qualified Dragon Hunter, but most dragons are much, much bigger than dogs.)

An important feature of all dragons is that their eyes face forward, which in the animal world means that they're hunters. Unlike some animals (for example, fish) that have eyes on the sides of their heads, dragons' eyes are close together, on the fronts of their faces.

Other animals' eyes also face forward. Think about a dog's eyes, or your own. Your eyes see the same thing at the same time. This is called *binocular* (bye-knock-you-ler) vision. Animals who have binocular vision are able to judge distances, which is very important when hunting for food. If a lion wants to chase a gazelle but can't tell how far away it is, he's going to have trouble.

The dragon's binocular vision is a great help when it needs to catch its prey. But since you also have binocular vision, you too can be a good hunter—of dragons.

28'
26'
24'
22'
20'
18'
16'
14'
12'
10'
8'
6'
4'
2'

1. CAN BE VERY LARGE IN SIZE
2. EYES FACE FORWARD
3. LARGE FANGS
4. SOME BREATHE FIRE
5. WINGS
6. SHORT ARMS

DRAGON CHARACTERISTICS: THOUGH FEATURES MAY VARY FROM DRAC

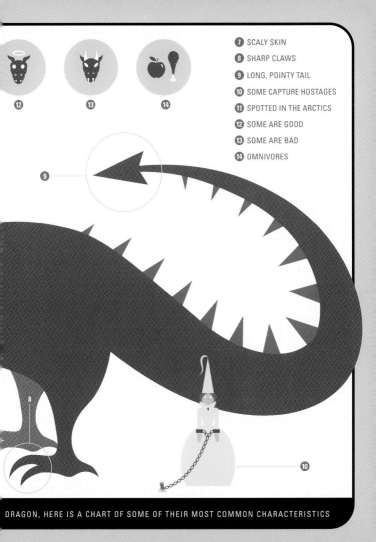

7 SCALY SKIN
8 SHARP CLAWS
9 LONG, POINTY TAIL
10 SOME CAPTURE HOSTAGES
11 SPOTTED IN THE ARCTICS
12 SOME ARE GOOD
13 SOME ARE BAD
14 OMNIVORES

DRAGON, HERE IS A CHART OF SOME OF THEIR MOST COMMON CHARACTERISTICS

MAMMAL OR REPTILE?

Dragon Hunters have debated how to classify dragons for many centuries. What sort of species are they? The answer boils down to a choice between mammal or reptile.

Mammals, which include dogs, cats, monkeys, and humans, are usually animals that live on land, although a few (like whales and dolphins) live in the ocean. They have hair or fur on their bodies and they don't lay eggs. They are also *warm-blooded,* which means that they keep a steady body temperature no matter how cold or hot the air is around them. For example, the average human's body temperature is 98.6°F. If you're outside in a snowstorm, your body temperature will still be 98.6°F. If you're lying on the beach under the hot sun, it will stay the same.

Reptiles, which include lizards, snakes, salamanders, and alligators, have scales instead of hair and lay eggs instead of giving birth to live babies. Reptiles are *cold-blooded,* which means that their body temperature changes to match their surroundings. If a snake goes outside in cold weather, its blood becomes as cold as the temperature outside, and the snake freezes. If it stays too long in the hot sun, its blood heats up and it gets too hot.

A dragon is a creature that falls somewhere between these two categories. Some of them have hair, but then again a lot of them have scales. All dragons lay eggs, but they're also warm-blooded. So which are they, mammal or reptile? It's difficult to be certain.

Dragons are not the first animals to be confusing in this way. Sharks are also hard to classify. With their rough skin, cartilage skeleton, and the ability to bear live young, they don't fit the definition for *any* animal group—not fish, not reptile, not mammal. They're a special kind of animal all their own that is neither reptile nor mammal, just shark. Dragons are also in a class all their own. Dragons are simply dragons.

GETTING TO KNOW THE DRAGON: FRIEND OR FOE?

Dragons, for the most part, are like people in that each has its own distinct personality. Not all dragons are angry or hostile. In fact, some are quite easy to get along with. Some of them are very intelligent, but others rely on instinct instead of thinking things through. For a Dragon Hunter, it is useful to group dragons into two categories: friendly and unfriendly.

A friendly dragon is, obviously, a lot easier to deal with. It will stay close to home, go out when it's hungry or bored, and usually won't cause trouble. If you ask it to, a friendly dragon will forage for food away from nearby cities or towns, where it might otherwise accidentally bump into and destroy houses. If it gets to know you well enough, you can even persuade a friendly dragon to be helpful. It may agree to transport you on its back to faraway places for visits. It may become protective and help keep away unfriendly dragons and other beasts. (This will only be possible after long association, so be patient.)

Beware of unfriendly dragons, however. They are hostile, bad-tempered, and prone to unprovoked attacks. Spotting an unfriendly dragon isn't difficult, because it usually leaves behind a trail of burned and crushed buildings, scared people, and large footprints. If an unfriendly dragon can find a suitable place to live that is far away from people, it might not be too much of a threat. Problems develop once the dragon is near people. Having a hostile dragon nearby that is capable of knocking things over and stepping on cars just isn't safe. As you'll read in Chapter 5, dealing with an unfriendly dragon is where you, the Dragon Hunter, come in.

ABILITIES AND TALENTS: WHAT CAN DRAGONS DO?

All dragons have special abilities. Some will have more than one ability, and the combinations are endless.

Many dragons can fly. All dragons have wings, but some have tiny wings that aren't strong enough to support them. A dragon is very heavy (an average-sized "large" dragon can weigh several tons) and needs big, muscular wings to allow it to get off the ground. Flying dragons are usually large, with massive, strong wings.

A dragon can also have magical abilities—the most powerful dragons can perform magic, not just do one special

DRAGON ABILITIES AND TALENTS

① FLIGHT | ② MAGIC | ③ SEE INTO THE FUTURE | ④ READ MINDS

⑤ SPEECH | ⑥ SENSE FEAR | ⑦ BREATHE FIRE

FLAMING BREATH: HOW DOES IT WORK?

Humans breathe *in* oxygen and breathe *out* carbon dioxide. A dragon is more like a plant or a tree: It breathes in carbon dioxide and breathes out oxygen. That oxygen is *flammable,* which means that it can easily catch on fire. In the back of the dragon's throat is a tiny spark, like a match, that it can light just by thinking about it. Here's how a dragon breathes fire:

1. The dragon takes a deep breath.

2. When breathing out, the dragon lights up the spark in the back of its throat.

3. The exhaled oxygen catches fire as it passes the spark.

4. The dragon opens its mouth and breathes out as hard as it can, propelling the jet of flames out of its mouth. Stand back! A dragon's jet of fire can reach up to fifty feet!

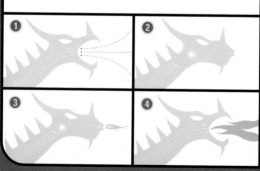

thing. Less powerful dragons can see the future, though the ones that can like to keep this ability a secret. A small percentage of dragons (perhaps 30 percent) also can read minds. Like the ability to see into the future, mind-reading is more common among intelligent, friendly dragons. A dragon that can read minds will often not tell you that it can, because this makes people uncomfortable. (Imagine if someone could hear all your thoughts!)

About 75 percent of dragons can speak fluently in the language native to the place where they were born. There are legends about a secret dragon language that humans can't understand, but we do not have any evidence of it. Dragons are also capable, just as humans are, of learning new languages.

All dragons, like dogs and bees, can sense fear. It's important for Dragon Hunters to control their emotions when near a dragon, especially if it's hostile. If it knows the hunter is afraid, a dragon might attack.

As many as 90 percent of dragons, according to popular legend, can breathe out fire. This is a very destructive talent in the hands of an unfriendly dragon, who can use it to wreak havoc wherever it goes.

DRAGON BEHAVIORS AND HABITS

When you are learning about any new kind of animal, one thing is always very important: the food the animal eats to stay alive. So what kinds of foods do dragons eat? Dragons, like people, are *omnivores* (om-nih-vohrz), which means that they eat both plants and meat.

The kinds of plants that humans eat—fruits and vegetables—are also what dragons eat. Most dragons don't like vegetables (can you blame them?), but they love fruit. It's sweet and nutritious and easy to find. A dragon easily picks apples off trees or tomatoes off plants. If a dragon does like vegetables, it'll usually stick with ones that it can get off the ground, like pumpkins or squash. Vegetables that grow underground are too difficult for a dragon to get a hold of: Its fingers are too large for digging!

A dragon will eat fruits and vegetables whole—even the skin! A lot of the vitamins in fruits and vegetables are contained in the skin, which we usually throw away, but dragons are so large that they need all the vitamins they can get, and dragons won't waste food if they can help it.

If fruits and vegetables are difficult to find, a dragon may resort to eating leaves off trees. This isn't their first choice, because the leaves don't really taste very good. But dragons need to eat greens just like humans do.

For meat, dragons often catch birds right out of the sky! Flying dragons can sneak up on a bird and gobble it up before the bird knows that the dragon is even there. If the dragon is in a hurry, it can eat while flying, but it would rather land, sit down, and enjoy the meal.

Dragons also love seafood. Seafood is tasty, satisfying, full of good nutrients, and it's relatively easy to find since, as you'll read below, almost all dragons live near bodies of water. Dragons have been seen wading in lakes and oceans

WHAT DRAGONS EAT

① FRUITS | ② VEGETABLES | ③ SEAFOOD | ④ MEAT | ⑤ LEAVES

trying to catch fish with their hands, the way people did before they had fishing poles. Unfortunately, despite their best efforts, dragons aren't very good at this. They splash about in the water and scare all the fish away. Most of the time, dragons have to be content with whatever fish washes up on the nearby shoreline.

If they live in forests or landlocked areas, dragons will hunt for their food. A dragon, despite its large size, can be surprisingly quiet when it wants to sneak up on an unsuspecting buffalo, bear, or deer. A big dragon can eat any of these animals in one sitting!

How often a dragon needs to eat depends on its size and on what it's eating. A small dragon, usually the size of a horse, doesn't need a lot of food, so it may eat its fill in the morning and not eat again for the rest of the day. A large dragon, which can be thirty feet tall with a twenty-foot tail, needs to eat more often, probably eating as much as it can two or three times a day.

DRAGONS: SOLITARY BEASTS OR SOCIAL BUTTERFLIES?

The dragon is mostly a solitary animal. It likes to be left alone, and it may feel threatened if too many dragons are nearby. Small dragons usually travel in packs, because having others around makes them feel safe and comfortable. Small dragons believe in safety in numbers, too.

As a general rule, the larger the dragon, the more of a loner it will be. A very large dragon is almost never seen living near other dragons. When big dragons are near each other, they end up competing for food and living space. It's easier to move farther away from each other than to start fighting over these things.

A DRAGON'S TERRITORY

A dragon, for the most part, is territorial. It will find a place to live and then stay there. It will protect its territory against other animals trying to move in—even unlucky humans who get too close. But how close is too close?

There aren't any hard and fast rules. Dragons don't mark their boundary lines like people do, with fences and walls. They simply protect any piece of land they consider theirs. Generally speaking, the larger the dragon, the larger the territory it guards.

Dragon experts believe that a dragon's territory extends as far as it can walk in a few minutes. Dragons don't like to claim more than they can protect, and if the land is too large, they can't guard it all at once. Estimates vary from dragon to dragon, but a dragon's territory is usually no more than two miles in any direction from its lair.

HABITAT REQUIREMENTS

Dragons need a nice, safe place to live where they'll be content and have what they need to live comfortably. In that way they're a lot like other animals, including humans. There are a few requirements every dragon has for a good lair:

1 WATER. Dragon lairs don't usually come with running water so they like to have a natural source of water nearby. Fresh water (a river or lake) is best, because ocean water is salty and not very satisfying.

2 GOOD CLIMATE. Dragons hate the heat and would rather be cold and shivery than hot and sweaty. Dragons gravitate to northern countries and away from places where it's warm all the time. They choose lairs that stay cool, like caves or shaded buildings.

3 VISTAS. Dragons like to live where they have a good view—like on the side of a mountain or on top of a hill. This might be because they can see trouble coming, but dragons may just like a pretty view.

A dragon's lair is its house, the home base where it lives and sleeps. The lair may be in a natural formation like a cave or an underground cavern. A dragon might also take up residence in a large abandoned building like a warehouse or a factory.

32'

CAUTION! A DRAGON WILL FEEL THREATENED IF YOU COME WITHIN 50 FEET OF ITS LAIR, AND IT WILL DEFEND ITSELF.

EXTINCT OR JUST HIDING?

Are dragons extinct? You and I know that they are not, or there would be no further need for Dragon Hunters. So why are dragon sightings around the world so rare?

Some experts speculate that the dragon isn't hiding—they claim that we see dragons all the time, but the dragons use magic to make us forget. Since not all dragons possess magic powers, this doesn't seem very likely.

Dragons may, however, have become more secretive as civilization has become more advanced. As more and more people cut down forests, build new cities and roads, and explore deep into the woods, dragons may have begun to hide so they wouldn't be hunted.

SOME EXPERTS CLAIM THAT DRAGONS MAY DATE BACK AS FAR AS PREHISTORIC TIMES, BUT SKEPTICS SAY THAT THOSE ARE JUST DINOSAURS.

CHAPTER TWO

DRAGON HISTORY

Almost all cultures have ancient legends and myths of dragons. Many dragon legends are so old, finding out when or where they started is difficult. The dragons of myth take many forms, some of which don't resemble what we think of as a dragon. In fact, the word "dragon" comes from the Greek word "draca," or "serpent," which perhaps indicates that dragons have evolved over time, from snakelike creatures into the beasts we now know.

The dragon has a long and glorious tradition in fairy tales, mythology, and folklore. Most of what we know of the dragon that doesn't come from observation comes from stories that were handed down from generation to generation. Some of them were first told thousands of years ago!

THE DRAGON IN CHINA

To the Chinese, the dragon is a very important creature. A long dragon puppet with many people inside is a common sight during Chinese New Year celebrations, and dragon symbols are very prominent in Chinese art.

There are nine major types of Chinese dragons, which, according to mythology, were the sons of the four Dragon Kings. Among these nine types were the Horned Dragon, the Celestial Dragon, the Yellow Dragon, and the Dragon of Hidden Treasures. The Chinese described the dragon's appearance as being made up of parts of other animals:

Horns of a deer • Head of a camel • Eyes of a devil
Neck of a snake • Stomach of a rooster • Scales of a fish
Claws of an eagle • Paws of a tiger • Ears of an ox

The Chinese people believed that the dragon had amazing powers, including the ability to bring rains and control floods. In history and lore, the dragon was responsible for guiding a person's spirit to the afterlife.

According to legend, dragons as well as evil spirits hate loud noises and are scared of blood—which is why firecrackers are set off during the Chinese New Year and why red is the traditional color of Chinese celebrations. These two deterrents—loud noises and the color red—may be helpful to you later, when you go hunting!

THE LEGEND OF SAINT GEORGE AND THE DRAGON

Saint George is one of the most famous saints of the Catholic Church, largely because of the legend of his battle with a dragon. Today, Saint George is both the official saint of England and the patron saint of the Boy Scouts of America.

George was a soldier in the army of the Roman Empire. No one is sure exactly when he lived, but it was probably more than 1,700 years ago. George decided to follow Christianity, which was still a new religion at the time. Christians back then were known as gentle and peaceful people, but George wanted to prove that a Christian could also be brave, so he decided to fight a dragon.

He found a dragon that had been destroying the countryside around a town called Cappadocia (kappa-doh-chee-ah) in ancient Turkey. The townspeople had tried to smooth things over with the dragon but nothing helped. Finally, the desperate citizens gave the dragon a young girl to see if it would stop attacking. This sacrifice didn't work, however, and the dragon kept on attacking.

Mounted on his majestic white horse, George charged the dragon. He killed it with a long lance (a sharp pole more than ten feet long) and rescued the damsel the dragon held captive. After that, knights all over the country took it upon themselves to fight dragons and rescue any hostages. (Since most of the captives were women, they were called "damsels in distress.") George wore a red cross on his shirt when he went into battle, and this symbol became the banner of England. Many Dragon Hunters celebrate Saint George's Feast Day, which is April 23.

BEOWULF AND THE DRAGON

Beowulf (bay-oh-wolf) is a famous king from an ancient English epic poem that is told in three parts. The third part tells of Beowulf's battle with a fire dragon. One of Beowulf's servants accidentally woke a fire dragon from its long sleep when he stole one of the dragon's trinkets. The dragon began setting fire to the countryside in Beowulf's kingdom. Beowulf, concerned for the safety of his subjects, resolved to rid the country of the dragon.

A young man named Wiglaf offered to help him, but Beowulf refused his assistance and went off to face the dragon alone. He challenged the dragon to come out of its lair and fight. The dragon tried to roast him with its fiery breath, but Beowulf's shield protected him. Beowulf tried to stab the dragon, but his sword broke, and before he could get another, the dragon fatally bit him.

Wiglaf, who had secretly followed Beowulf, rushed forward and killed the dragon, then held Beowulf in his arms until the dragon's poison killed him. Before he died, Beowulf gave Wiglaf his crown and broken sword and declared him the new king.

OTHER FAMOUS DRAGONS IN HISTORY

THE HYDRA

The half-god hero Hercules was given twelve labors to perform, the second of which was to fight the Hydra. The Hydra was a huge dragonlike creature with nine heads, one of which was immortal. Hercules soon discovered the difficult part: For each head that he sliced off, two grew in its place. He finally defeated the beast by

cutting off the immortal head and burying it underneath a rock to make sure no one else could ever be hurt by it. (This battle is shown in part in the Disney version of Hercules's story.)

FAFNIR

Fafnir is a dragon of Norse mythology who appears in stories told by the Vikings in what is today Norway, Sweden, and Finland. This dragon was killed by the hero Siegfried to gain the treasure that Fafnir guarded.

THE PIASA

This dragon comes from Native American legend, specifically the Algonquin tribe. The Piasa had a dragon's body, a human's face, and a lion's mane. According to legend, the Piasa lived near the Mississippi River and kidnapped humans for food until Ouatoga, the chief, with the help of twenty warriors, killed it.

SMAUG

Smaug is a fictional dragon in J. R. R. Tolkien's classic fantasy story *The Hobbit*. The dragon guarded the Dwarven treasures buried in Lonely Mountain.

THE DRAGON TODAY

Dragons still appear frequently in the literature and entertainment of today's culture, though these portrayals may not necessarily reflect reality. Real tales of dragon sightings still occur. Some Dragon Hunters wonder if the legendary Loch Ness Monster is really a type of aquatic dragon.

DRAGON IMPOSTORS

There are a number of animals today that are sometimes mistaken for dragons, nearly all of which are reptiles. Examples include the Komodo dragon, which lives in the Galapagos Islands; crocodiles and alligators, which are native to many tropical climates; and the Gila monster, the largest lizard in the United States. Recognizing the tracks of these animals and comparing them to actual dragon tracks is an important exercise for a Dragon Hunter.

IDENTIFYING TRACKS

1 **KOMODO DRAGON** (Varanus komodoensis) 10' in length

2 **ALLIGATOR** (Alligator mississippiensis) 12' in length

3 **IGUANA** (Iguana iguana) 6' in length

4 **GILA MONSTER** (Heloderma suspectum) 2' in length

5 **CROCODILE** (Crocodylus niloticus) 16' in length

6 **DRAGON** (Draco sapientis) 25' in length

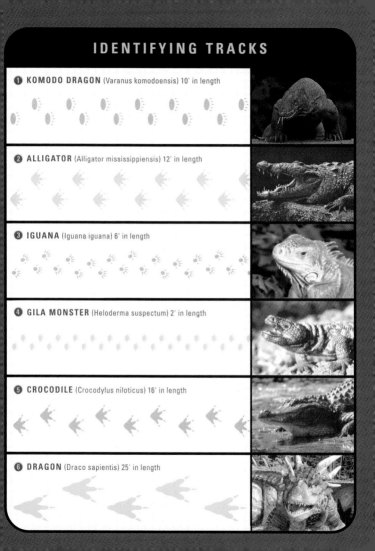

FIRE EXTINGUISHER

SWORD

SHIELD

ARMOR

KNOCKOUT DROPS

NET

CHAPTER THREE

DRAGON HUNTING

Dragon hunting is a time-honored profession dating back thousands of years. There were probably Dragon Hunters well before the first dragon stories started making the rounds. (The first stories are set in ancient Greece in about 1000 B.C.)

As a Dragon Hunter, you'll need to be enthusiastic, eager for a challenge, ready to use your head, and above all else, well prepared. Anything can happen!

In the past, Dragon Hunters were like policemen. Every town had a local Dragon Hunter who was usually paid in food, lodging, clothing, or even money. These days, Dragon Hunters view hunting dragons more as a hobby than as a profession.

So what sorts of things might you find yourself doing as a Dragon Hunter? Well, hunting, of course. Tracking and following dragons is an important part of the job. If friendly dragons are in your area, observe them.

You might also find yourself negotiating with friendly dragons, dealing with dragons that don't feel like moving away from human habitats, and even helping to spread warnings about dangerous dragons moving into an area.

It's impossible to anticipate just what you'll be doing as a Dragon Hunter. Be ready for the unexpected, and remember to use your head!

EQUIPMENT

All Dragon Hunters need a significant amount of equipment to start out. The basic list includes:

1. **TRANSPORTATION.** You may find yourself walking and running a great deal as you follow a dragon's trail. If you have to go farther or faster, and you know how to ride, a horse might be a good choice. If you don't, then a bicycle is a great way to get around quickly. You can even use a skateboard or a scooter.

2. **PROTECTIVE CLOTHING.** When dealing with hostile, fire-breathing dragons, you need to protect your skin, including your arms, legs, and hands. Thick leather works well. It should cover all your skin but allow you freedom to move. The legendary Dragon Hunters wore metal armor, but this can be really heavy and gets super-hot when jets of fire get near it! Pick a fabric like denim (jeans)

or cotton. Man-made fabrics like polyester are highly flammable and too dangerous for a Dragon Hunter. If you can wear red, do so. It's the classic color of Dragon Hunters since dragons *hate* the color red!

③ **A HEAT-RESISTANT SHIELD.** Ceramic shields are best, but they can be heavy and awkward. The most useful shields can be found around the house. A large lid from a cooking pot or a large tray are both effective. A metal trash can lid can also be effective, but it will get hot quickly. Be sure to wear gloves!

④ **WEAPONS.** Swords are the weapons of choice for many hunters, but they have the disadvantage that you must be close to the dragon to use one. Therefore, most modern hunters like to use slingshots and high-pressure water pistols. Darts poisoned with knockout drops are also great weapons.

KNOCKOUT DROPS AT HOME

Dragon knockout drops are indispensable. They put the dragon to sleep so you can transport it safely. Either you can put the liquid on darts or you can immobilize the dragon (more on this later) and then spray drops near its nose.

These drops are not dangerous to humans, but whatever you do, don't drink any yourself. They really taste awful.

1 cup apple juice
10 drops Tabasco sauce
5 drops green food coloring
1/2 cup vinegar

Mix well, pour mixture into an empty spray bottle, and screw on the cap tightly. Shake vigorously, and the drops are ready for use.

⑤ **FIRE EXTINGUISHERS.** You can never have too many of these. Place a small one on your belt and a larger one in your knapsack. Make sure the extinguisher is easy to grab, and be ready to use it at the slightest sign of fiery breath.

⑥ **COMFORTABLE SHOES.** These are never a bad idea, especially when you'll be walking a great deal! After all, dragons don't usually live right next door.

⑦ **ROPE.** This is an effective tool for disabling a dragon, because you can use it to tie the dragon's legs together. Make sure to carry a good amount of sturdy rope.

⑧ **A LARGE NET.** Once a dragon is on the ground (more on this later), throwing a net over it keeps it from getting back up and allows you to move it to a safe location.

⑨ **A COMPASS.** You may be tracking the dragon over some distance, and you need to keep your bearings.

⑩ **MAPS OF THE AREA.** These can help you anticipate where the dragon might go and help you to decide on the best way to follow it.

⑪ **WATER.** Always take along a canteen or sports bottle full of water. You will get lots of exercise as you walk or run after the dragon, and you'll get thirsty.

⑫ **A KNAPSACK OR BAG TO CARRY YOUR SUPPLIES.** A sturdy leather or canvas pack, even a backpack, can carry your supplies and keep your hands free.

⑬ **YOUR DRAGON HUNTER'S HANDBOOK,** of course!

① ② BIG BRIGHT EYES

③ NON-THREATENING HORNS ON HEAD   ④ OFTEN SEEN SMILING OR GRINNING

THE FRIENDLY DRAGON

The friendly dragon, as you might imagine, will cause you a lot fewer headaches than the unfriendly one. Spotting a friendly dragon is quite simple: If it hasn't attacked anyone or burned anything down, it's probably friendly. You should still approach with caution, however, and never assume a dragon is friendly just from outward appearances.

BUILDING A RELATIONSHIP

Before you can deal effectively with a friendly dragon, you need to establish a relationship. In many ways, making friends with a dragon isn't much different from making friends with people. If the dragon is able to speak, communication can be easy. Even if the dragon cannot speak, however, it can still understand you, so the way to deal with a non-speaking dragon is the same. Smiling, for instance, or making friendly gestures can communicate as much as words.

Begin by approaching the dragon in a non-threatening manner. Walk with your head held high—smile! Hold out your hands so the dragon can see that you're unarmed.

Introduce yourself as you would to a new friend. Say hello, and tell the dragon your name. Remember to treat the dragon with respect at all times. Dragons can be very sensitive. Don't make jokes or sarcastic comments. If the dragon can speak, it may tell you its name. Most friendly dragons react well to friendly overtures from humans.

Let the dragon set the pace for developing a friendship. If the dragon has been lonely, it may be excited to meet someone new and want to talk with you for a long time. Or, it may prefer to see you only for a few minutes at a time. Remember, dragons are bigger than you, so don't push your luck!

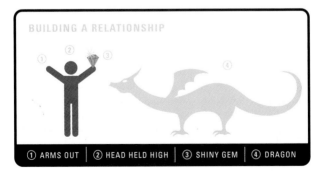

BUILDING A RELATIONSHIP

① ARMS OUT | ② HEAD HELD HIGH | ③ SHINY GEM | ④ DRAGON

Treat the dragon as you would a new friend. Offer to spend time with it, or show it some of the sights of your city. Bring gifts. Dragons like shiny things and may appreciate a gift of polished stones or prisms.

Once you've established a relationship with the dragon and it considers you a friend, you may arrange for it to be a town's protector. You may also ask it to do favors for you. Remember, though, that dragons can get angry if they think that you're friends with them only because you want something. Wouldn't you? Remember the golden rule: Treat the dragon as you would want to be treated.

WHAT IF THE DRAGON GETS TOO ATTACHED TO YOU?

Some dragons form close attachments to children. They have been known to follow their friend after a move and even come to their aid in times of danger. This might seem fine, but consider the consequences of having a thirty-foot dragon following you everywhere you go!

Having a dragon as a friend can be great, and humans can become very attached to their dragon friends as well. However, you should make sure your friend understands that there is a time and a place for a dragon in your life, and for you in its life.

But if having a dragon follow you around doesn't bother you, then there's no problem. A dragon can make a wonderful friend as long as you're careful that it doesn't accidentally knock over your neighbor's house with its tail.

THE VILLAGE PROTECTOR

In fairy tales and legends of old, a friendly dragon usually ends up being the village protector. Some more modern and intelligent dragons object to this portrayal, making the valid point that dragons don't exist just to watch out for humans. On the other hand, there are plenty of friendly dragons that happily fill this role and protect their towns out of affection and a sense of duty.

EXCHANGE OF GOODS AND SERVICES FOR PROTECTION

① FOOD | ② FIREWOOD | ③ PROTECTION FROM ANGRY MOBS

The key here is to listen to the dragon's wishes. If the dragon feels good when it protects your town, let it. If your local friendly dragon isn't inclined to be protective, it may be willing to assume that role in exchange for goods or services: food, firewood, protection from angry mobs of people, and so on.

But if your local dragon isn't interested in being a protector, don't push it. Just be grateful it isn't an unfriendly dragon that might burn down your town.

WISH-GRANTING

In rare cases, friendly dragons have the magical ability to grant wishes. A note of caution: Some deceptive dragons have been known to claim wish-granting ability when they don't actually have it. Don't expect too much, and don't be surprised if it isn't true.

WISHING GUIDELINES

TO HELP YOU MAKE SMARTER WISHES, CONSIDER THESE TIPS:

1 AVOID ONE-TIME WISHES.
Instead of wishing for an object, wish for the ability to get that thing for yourself. For example, if you are tempted to wish for a trip to Paris, wish instead for a pilot and private jet of your very own. That way you can go to Paris whenever you want. Instead of wishing for good grades on your next test, wish for the discipline to study harder so you can get good grades all the time.

2 DON'T WISH TO BE BETTER THAN SOMEONE ELSE.
Too often, these wishes are granted by making the other person worse off than before. You don't want your wishes to come at the expense of someone else. If you wish to be a faster runner than Johnny, the wish may be granted by making Johnny break his leg! Do you really want that? If you want to be a better runner, wish for *yourself* to get better.

3 DON'T WISH FOR MORE WISHES.
This will likely just make the dragon mad. Dragons hate it when people try to outsmart them, so just use the wish(es) you're given and be grateful you got any at all.

Wish-granting is usually done either out of gratitude for a service you have done for the dragon or in exchange for something the dragon needs or wants. Either way, the offer should not be taken lightly. The dragon may determine how many wishes to grant, but be advised that certain wishes may be beyond the dragon's power. It may be able to give you money, but it might not be able to make someone fall in love with you or transport you to Florida. The dragon also reserves the right to refuse any wishes that it thinks are wrong or impossible. Wish-granting dragons take their abilities very seriously and won't refuse a wish request for petty reasons.

The old advice is doubly true here: Be careful what you wish for. Be very clear with your words and be as specific as possible. Legends are full of people who made ill-advised wishes for things they thought they wanted and end up regretting it.

WHEN WISHES GO WRONG

Once there was a king named Midas. He was granted a wish, and he wished that everything he touched would turn to gold. It was granted, and the king was delighted. He went around touching things and turning them to gold. It seemed like he would never need money again. But then he found out that his gift wasn't all good. He touched his food, and it turned to solid gold! He touched his children, and they turned to gold, too. Midas was horrified. The wish he thought he wanted instead made him very unhappy.

① KING MIDAS | ②③④ DAUGHTER, DINNER, AND DOG TURNED TO GOLD

1. **POINTY HORNS ON HEAD**   2. **SQUINTY EYES**

3. **ALWAYS SNARLS OR GROWLS**   4. **LARGE, SCARY LOOKING MOUTH**

CHAPTER FIVE

THE UNFRIENDLY DRAGON

And so we come to perhaps the most important part of this handbook, the area all good Dragon Hunters must be familiar with: dealing with unfriendly dragons.

Such dragons are generally easy to spot. A dragon that will attack people or homes is probably unfriendly, but you shouldn't jump immediately to that conclusion. The dragon may have been provoked.

Check around. Ask the local townspeople if anyone has been bothering the dragon or if someone has attacked it. If that's the case, your job is to find the dragon, calm it down, and try your best to fix the problem. If the dragon was not provoked, it's a dangerous animal and must be dealt with promptly.

SPOTTING THE UNFRIENDLY DRAGON: WARNING SIGNS

Ninety-nine percent of unfriendly dragons are large enough to be easily spotted, so this is not as difficult as it may sound. In fact, if a dragon were on the rampage, it would be difficult *not* to hear about it, because people will talk about a sighting. Dragon attacks are serious, scary, and leave many telltale signs.

SIGNS OF DRAGON ATTACKS

① SCORCH MARKS (ON ROADS, TREES, WALLS, ETC.) AND BURNED BUILDINGS

② HOMES DESERTED IN A HURRY (DOORS LEFT OPEN, MEALS HALF EATEN, TVS LEFT ON)

③ FOOD STORAGE AREAS LOOTED (GRAIN SILOS, SUPERMARKETS, BUTCHER SHOPS)

④ LARGE FOOTPRINTS

⑤ TREES AND SMALL BUILDINGS BLOWN OVER BY THE WIND FROM THE DRAGON'S WINGS

⑥ CLAW MARKS IN SURFACES LIKE WALLS, FLOORS, AND STREETS

PURSUING THE UNFRIENDLY DRAGON

You can use some of the signs mentioned above to track a dragon, but often your most helpful resource will be word of mouth. A dragon is too large to travel unnoticed, and if you can determine which way it went (from footprints or eyewitness accounts), you can usually follow it without too much trouble. If that fails, look for leftovers from its meals, footprints, blown-down trees, and scorched vegetation or buildings.

WILL THEY LISTEN TO REASON?

The short answer to this question is: No. Generalizations are never completely accurate, but trying to reason with a hostile dragon is nearly impossible. It's unproductive and wastes valuable time.

However, if a dragon is attacking because it was provoked, it may listen to reason. No matter if the dragon is friendly or unfriendly, many dragons have quick tempers and can fly into a rage easily. The difference is that a friendly dragon will regret its outburst and listen to you if you ask it to stop, especially if there has been a misunderstanding that you can explain. An unfriendly dragon will feel no remorse and can be virtually unstoppable.

Most of the time, a hostile dragon is just that: hostile. As unpleasant as it is to admit, some dragons are unfriendly by nature and can't be reasoned with.

EVIL DRAGONS ARE NOTORIOUS FOR LEAVING

BEHIND A PATH OF DESTRUCTION, AS CAN BE SEEN IN THESE DISASTERS

CONFRONTING THE UNFRIENDLY DRAGON

Rule number one for these confrontations is BE CAREFUL. A hostile dragon is unpredictable and angry. The best way to confront it is to first wait for it to calm down. No dragon can keep up a high energy level for hours at a time, so soon after attacking it will tire and need to rest. This is the best time to move in and try to deal with the situation.

If you must confront a dragon during an attack—which is not recommended but is sometimes necessary—DO NOT corner it. If you force it into a situation from which retreat is impossible, it will become even more hostile. Leave it a way to escape and it won't turn on you quite so quickly. Try to lead it away from people and homes and into a secluded area. Most dragons will recognize a Dragon Hunter when they see one, from your clothing, shield, and confident manner. This means that they'll just want to chase *you* instead of innocent townspeople. Luckily, you'll be prepared for this. Try to get the dragon to chase you to an isolated area without trees.

ALWAYS KEEP YOUR DISTANCE DURING A CONFRONTATION

If you get the dragon away from whatever or whomever it's attacking, it will probably calm down a little bit, at least enough for you to confront it.

BRIBERY

Dragons can be just as greedy as humans and will attack because they need or want something. If you offer a bribe, usually food, and promise to keep the dragon supplied for as long as it stops attacking, you may be able to stop the attacks without any violence.

This approach works best if you offer the dragon a type of food it has a hard time getting. Dragons love fish, but catching any is hard because of their size, so seafood is a great bribe. Many dragons also have a sweet tooth, so molasses or sugar can also be useful bribes—and few dragons would turn down a gallon of ice cream!

The catch is that the townspeople must be willing to participate in this arrangement. You can't stick around forever, so if you want the dragon to stay happy, the people who live nearby will have to be the ones who keep it supplied with fish or sugar (or whatever you've promised). If they don't hold up their part of the bargain, the dragon may become even more hostile because it will feel (rightly) cheated out of the agreement.

In many legends, dragons were keepers of great treasures. Gold, jewels, and other valuables would lie deep within a dragon's lair, rarely seen by human eyes. Any dragon with such a stash would gladly accept more trinkets!

WHAT TO DO
IF THINGS GO BADLY

Sometimes the dragon can't be talked down, can't be led away, can't be bribed, or can't be bargained with. This is a very dangerous situation that will require the following emergency measures:

1. Get people far away from the dragon—as quickly as possible. Make sure all buildings are evacuated.

2. Enlist the help of the local police and anyone else willing to search the entire town so no one is left behind.

3. Send messages to nearby towns that a dangerous dragon is on the loose. They should be ready to evacuate.

4. Try to contact any other Dragon Hunters that may be in the area for help.

5. Make a lot of noise. Get local Dragon Hunters to start banging on trash cans, shouting, anything they can do

to make a lot of noise. The dragon will likely want to get away from the loud noises and will leave.

⑥ Prepare your weapons and make sure you are protected from harm. If the noise does not faze the dragon, you will have to do battle with it.

SELF-DEFENSE TECHNIQUES

If you must do battle with a dragon, be prepared to defend yourself. If you can, work with another Dragon Hunter: He or she can perform the same moves, which will further disorient the dragon. Two hunters are always better than one!

① Move quickly and dart around so the dragon will have trouble catching you. Dragons aren't very quick due to their large size. Try to be a moving target, and crouch down to make yourself appear as small as possible.

SELF-DEFENSE TECHNIQUES

① CONFUSE THE DRAGON BY RUNNING AROUND ｜ ② RUN BENEATH ITS LEG

④ MAKE SURE DRAGON DOES NOT FLY AWAY

② Dragons get dizzy easily because their heads are so far off the ground. Duck back and forth between their legs or around their backs, forcing them to turn around rapidly. The dragon may get disoriented and fall down, at which point you can easily tranquilize or net it.

③ Keep your shield in front of you at all times. It can be used to deflect claws, tails, or bursts of fire. If attacked, keep your face behind the shield and hold it on your forearm for maximum leverage.

④ Keep the dragon from taking flight. You can only fight it if it's on the ground; once it takes off and flies away you must pursue it and repeat the entire process. The good news is that once a dragon is fighting with a person, its attention is so focused that it usually forgets to fly away.

⑤ Get the dragon onto the ground. Making it dizzy or encircling its legs with rope can cause the dragon to stumble and fall. Once it's down, throw the net over the dragon. Then administer knockout drops or try to spray a fire extinguisher into its mouth. The extinguisher will render its firepower useless for at least a few hours.

RESCUING HOSTAGES

When the dragon is holding a hostage, an entirely new element enters the fight. Now your primary objective is not to neutralize the dragon, but to rescue the innocent person. A dragon will fiercely protect a hostage, so this can be very difficult.

To be successful, you must work with another Dragon Hunter. Have your partner engage the dragon and lure it away from the hostage while you sneak in and free the captive. If another Dragon Hunter is not available, an able-bodied and quick person from the town can sometimes assist you, but as the Dragon Hunter you should be the one engaging the dragon.

If you cannot work as a team, this task becomes more difficult but is still possible. You will need to be quick. The strategy is still similar, except you will have to perform both tasks yourself.

(1) Engage the dragon. Shout at it, run around in circles, do anything you can to get its attention. The dragon will advance toward you.

(2) Move slowly but steadily backward, away from the hostage. The dragon will follow you.

(3) Start weaving around to confuse the dragon.

(4) Run quickly to the hostage and free him or her. Be ready to turn and fight off the dragon as the hostage runs away.

(5) Follow the steps in Self-Defense Techniques (pp. 69–73) to neutralize the dragon.

RESCUING THE HOSTAGE

① ENGAGE THE DRAGON | ② MOVE SLOWLY BACKWARD | ③ CONFUSE THE DRAGON

④ SET HOSTAGE FREE | ⑤ NEUTRALIZE THE DRAGON

THE LAST RESORT

Your goal in dealing with a hostile dragon should be to find a way to stop it from attacking. If there is no way, you may have no choice but to kill it. This, however, should be your last resort. Dragons have a right to live just like any other animal, and you should try to avoid killing them.

One alternative may be to stun the dragon and then transport it to a remote location (see p. 78) where it may live peacefully, away from human contact. There are a number of places where a hostile dragon may be taken. They are remote and offer everything a dragon could want, so it won't want to return to your town.

Transporting a large dragon can be tricky. Try to get the dragon to fall by making it dizzy or by binding its legs with rope, then throw a net over it and administer a large dose of knockout drops. Once it's asleep, you'll need to transport it. At this point, you'll need the help of a trusted adult. Some Dragon Hunters hire helicopters, but this is rather conspicuous. It may be better to rent a large truck.

If you absolutely cannot transport the dragon because of its size, or if the dragon is too hostile to be controlled long enough to be subdued for travel, you may have no choice but to neutralize it permanently. Dragons have a vulnerable spot below their necks. It's a soft area without scales or hair where they take in oxygen. If a dragon is wounded in that spot, it cannot survive for long.

Use a slingshot to launch something small (a dart or sharp stone) that has been doused in knockout drops at the vulnerable area. Aim carefully!

Killing the dragon is only acceptable after you've exhausted all other options. Killing dragons indiscriminately is considered dishonorable among Dragon Hunters.

SAFE PLACES FOR
DRAGON REFUGE

1. ALASKA
2. SASKATCHEWAN, CANADA
3. GREENLAND
4. ICELAND
5. NORWAY
6. NORTHERN FINLA...

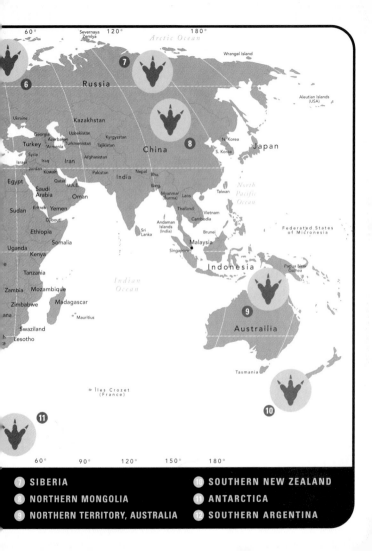

CONCLUSION

Whether you've just made a large, scaly friend or you've managed to free a city of its fire-breathing menace, you now know you've got all it takes to be a true Dragon Hunter.

Not only that—you've also learned some important skills that you can teach others. Like the generations of Dragon Hunters that have come before you, you can pass the tactics and tips you've learned to a whole new generation of modern hunters. The more people know about the basic rules of identifying, befriending, defending against, and—most of all—*understanding* dragons, the safer all of us will be.

Be proud! You've joined the ranks of the greatest Dragon Hunters of all time. Like them, you have a very important quality: courage. And courage, along with the know-how you've learned in this book, is all you'll need to contend with any and all dragons that cross your path.

Remember to keep an eye out for any unexplained destruction in your town and surroundings: fires that have no known source, a collapsed building that seemed structurally sound, and so on. As you've learned, these may be telltale signs that a dragon lives or has lived nearby. Use the special Dragon Hunter's Notebook on pages 84–85 to record your clues and sightings. Having your written account will help you compare notes with your fellow Dragon Hunters.

Armed with your homemade knockout drops, your quick feet, and your *Dragon Hunter's Handbook*, you're ready to put all you've learned into action.

Good luck, and good hunting!

APPENDIX: FURTHER READING AND VIEWING

BOOKS

There are a lot of great books that feature dragons. Here are a few to get you started.

The Dragon Chronicles (series) by Susan Fletcher (1991–1996)

Dragonriders of Pern (series) by Anne McCaffrey (1971–1979)

Dragons: A Natural History by Dr. Karl Shuker (1995)

Harry Potter and the Goblet of Fire by J. K. Rowling (2000)

Here There Be Dragons by Jane Yolen (1993)

The Lord of the Rings trilogy by J. R. R. Tolkien (1954–1955)

The Neverending Story by Michael Ende (1976)

MOVIES

Dragons have also appeared on the silver screen many times. Rent one of these to see a dragon in action.

Dragonheart, directed by Rob Cohen (1996)

Dragonslayer, directed by Rob Cohen (1979)

Dungeons and Dragons, directed by Courtney Solomon (2000)

The Lord of the Rings: The Fellowship of the Ring,
    directed by Peter Jackson (2001)

Mulan, directed by Tony Bancroft/Barry Cook (1998)

The Neverending Story, directed by Wolfgang Petersen (1984)

Pete's Dragon, directed by Don Chaffey (1977)

Sleeping Beauty, directed by Clyde Geronimi (1959)

WEBSITES

Find other dragon fans on-line: Check out these websites.

The Adopt-A-Dragon Foundation:
www.camalott.com/~malathar/adfmain.html

Here There Be Dragons:
www.draconian.com

**The Renaissance Entertainment Corporation
(Renaissance fairs):** www.renfair.com

Alt.fan.dragons Web site:
www.dragonfire.org

DRAGON HUNTER'S NOTEBOOK

SIGHTING DATE:

SIGHTING TIME:

LOCATION:

DRAGON APPEARANCE:

HEIGHT:

WEIGHT:

COLOR:

SCALES OR HAIR:

FIRE-BREATHING (YES/NO):

FLYING (YES/NO):

VISIBLE EVIDENCE:

◯ SCORCHED BUILDINGS   ◯ CLAW MARKS ON BUILDINGS

◯ CLAW MARKS ON ROADS   ◯ DOWNED TREES AND BUILDINGS

DRAGON ASSESSMENT:

◯ FRIENDLY   ◯ UNFRIENDLY

COMMENTS:

DRAGON HUNTER IDENTIFICATION

FORTES FORTUNA JUVAT

Fortune Favors the Brave

The bearer of this ID has read and understood *The Dragon Hunter's Handbook*, and is well-equipped to deal with even the most hostile of dragons. The bearer understands and can easily spot the difference between an unfriendly and a friendly dragon—and knows how to deal with both.

The bearer should be allowed into any wooded regions uncharted by humans, into scenes of apparent natural disaster, and will act as a liaison between the dragon and any nearby townspeople.